ZZLE PIRATES

Susannah Leigh

Illustrated by Brenda Haw

Contents

Edited by Jenny Tyler
Design co-ordinator: Laura Parker

About this book

This book is about a boy named Joe who is learning how to be a pirate at school. Before he can be a real pirate, Joe must earn his pirate cutlass. There is a puzzle to solve on every double page. If you get stuck, the answers are on pages 31 and 32.

Pirate School has finished for the summer when Joe gets an exciting message from his uncle, Buccaneer Bill. Bill is no ordinary uncle. He is a pirate, and the message sounds serious.

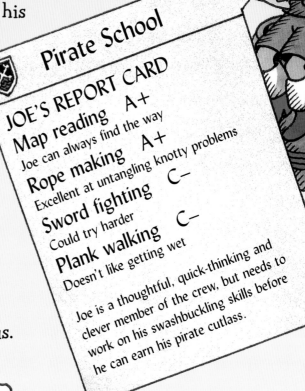

Joe

Pirate School

JOE'S REPORT CARD

Map reading   A+
Joe can always find the way

Rope making   A+
Excellent at untangling knotty problems

Sword fighting   C−
Could try harder

Plank walking   C−
Doesn't like getting wet

Joe is a thoughtful, quick-thinking and clever member of the crew, but needs to work on his swashbuckling skills before he can earn his pirate cutlass.

Ahoy there, Joe!

Great news – I've found a treasure map! Trouble is, me old foe, Captain Cutthroat overheard me bragging about the treasure. Off that sneaky seadog sailed with his band of scurvy brigands and I haven't seen him since. They're looking for the treasure too, no doubt. Luckily I still have the map, but I need some help. Come and put your pirate school skills to the test on my new ship, the Salty Seal, and help me find that treasure before Captain Cutthroat.
Meet me at Pirate's Port tomorrow.

Love from your Uncle, Buccaneer Bill x

Joe has heard of Captain Cutthroat. He leads his pirate crew around the high seas, stealing and fighting and generally being bad. Joe can't wait to help Uncle Bill and find the treasure before Cutthroat gets to it.

Captain Cutthroat

Bill

Careful who you tell about that map, Bill. Loose lips sink ships y'know.

Things to spot

Joe is excited, but a little worried too. He hasn't been at pirate school long, and his pirate skills need work. But he is very observant. There are lots of things to look out for on the voyage. See if you can help him by spotting one thing on every double page.

octopus

maggot

angry porcupine

hungry crocodile

ghostly pirate

giant rat

jellyfish

stinging wasp

toothy starfish

shark

skull

bald gull

spiky puffer fish

Spot the parrot

Uncle Bill has a parrot named Colin. Colin is a little shy, but you can find him on every double page if you look carefully.

Mermaids' purses

There is a mermaid's purse on every double page. Can you spot them all? Maybe you will find some mermaids along the way to give them to!

3

Search for the Salty Seal

The next day, Joe skipped down to Pirate's Port to find Uncle Bill's ship, the Salty Seal. Luckily, Uncle Bill had sent him a drawing of the ship, so it should be easy to spot.

But when he arrived at the sea, Joe saw there were lots of boats and ships bobbing around. Which one was the Salty Seal?

Can you spot the Salty Seal?

Watch out for Cutthroat's Ghastly Galleon!

My boat, the Salty Seal.

SIZE 12

BARREL
OF LIMES

SAILS 4
SALE

All aboard!

Joe found a little boat and rowed across to the Salty Seal. Uncle Bill beamed down at him.

"Ahoy there, Joe! You made it. Now, climb aboard!"

Joe gazed at the maze of ropes and ladders that covered the side of the ship. How would he ever climb up?

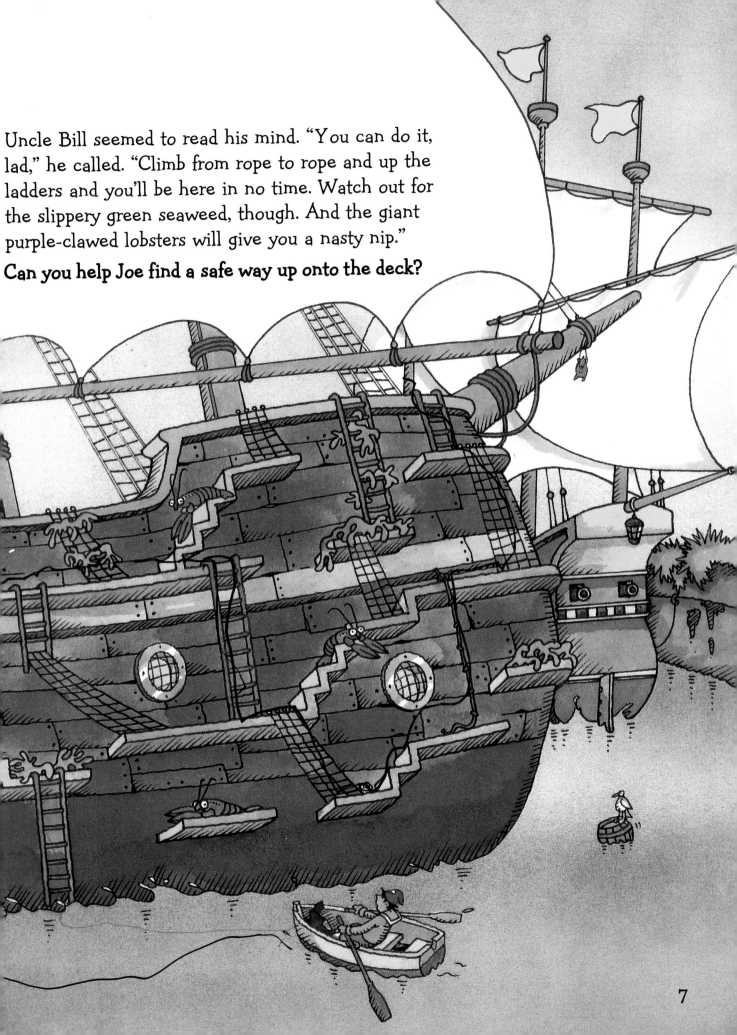

Uncle Bill seemed to read his mind. "You can do it, lad," he called. "Climb from rope to rope and up the ladders and you'll be here in no time. Watch out for the slippery green seaweed, though. And the giant purple-clawed lobsters will give you a nasty nip."

Can you help Joe find a safe way up onto the deck?

Meet the crew

Joe pulled himself up the last ladder and clambered over the rail, landing in an exhausted heap at Uncle Bill's feet. Uncle Bill picked him up in his beefy arms and gave him a swashbuckling sque-e-e-e-e-ze.

"Oo arr, Joe, am I glad to see you," he boomed. "Now, meet me crew!" Bill gestured to a motley band of pirates. "They're all new recruits like you, and I'm still learning their names. Let's see, who is who?"

Look carefully at the pirates' names. Can you help Joe decide who is who?

There's Peg-leg Poll and Mophead Mick, One-eyed Jem and Rufus Redhead. Oh, and don't forget Stripes, the ship's cat.

8

Treasure map

Joe guessed everyone's names correctly. Then the ladders, ropes and nets on the side of the ship were pulled up and the Salty Seal was ready to set sail. Bill sat Joe down at the captain's table and spread out a big map before him.

"We've got to set a course for Deadly Isle," Bill explained. "That's where the treasure is buried. The instructions are written on the map, but me old pirate brain ain't as quick as she used to be. Can ye help me find Deadly Isle, Joe?"

Can you follow the clues to find Deadly Isle?

Clues :

N W E S

Start at port and sail North East –
To the red ragged rocks, then East to the beast.
On to pink seaweed cove, then North to Green Land,
West from there and you're close at hand.
With the yellow-tailed dolphins, play awhile
Then North West past a monster to Deadly Isle!

Sea voyage

Joe helped Bill to plot a course for Deadly Isle. Several yo ho hos later, the Salty Seal set sail on the search for treasure. Uncle Bill was at the wheel. Joe, who was good at map reading, was navigating.

Together they journeyed...

...through windy weather

and stormy seas...

...past watery creatures

and playful friends,

until at last —

"Land ahoy! Deadly Isle – dead ahead!"
"Ye did it lad, ye led us here!" cried Bill.
Joe felt as pleased as pirate punch. But as
he took a closer look at Deadly Isle, he
spotted something he had seen earlier that
day. Something that made his heart sink to
the bottom of his boots.

**What has Joe spotted, and who does it
belong to?**

Rocky reefs

Uncle Bill's face went as purple as a parrot's plume. "How in barnacles did Cutthroat get here first?"

Joe took a closer look at the ship. "I can't see anyone on board," he said. "Cutthroat must be ashore."

"Let's get there and find the treasure, then," Bill cried.

Joe smiled. "I've got a better plan. Launch our row boat, Uncle Bill. We're going aboard that ship."

14

"I may only have one eye," said Jem,
"but even I can see the rocky reefs in the way."

"Let's get through them quickly," said Joe.
"I have this strange feeling we're being watched..."

**Can you find a safe way through the rocky reefs
to Cutthroat's ship? Some of the rocks have eyes –
can you see how many?**

15

Joe's plan

Safely through the rocky reefs, Joe tried to tell everyone his plan. But the wind was whistling and his words were blown away.

Can you put the pictures in the right order and discover Joe's plan?

First, we'll all row to the Ghastly Galleon,

Meanwhile, Mophead and I will row behind the Galleon,

and when the ship is at sea, we will pick you up.

We might meet Cutthroat and his crew there, but with their ship out to sea, they'll be stranded!

Then we'll all row back to Deadly Isle to look for the treasure.

where Bill, Rufus, Jem and Peg will climb aboard and set sail.

Deadly Isle

Joe's plan worked! They were ashore Deadly Isle, with Cutthroat's ship far out to sea. Just then, there was a rustle in the bushes.

"Cutthroat!" Bill hissed.

"No, worse!" yelled Joe as a band of bone-shaking pirate skeletons lurched towards them, teeth grinning and swords slashing.

"Now I know why they call this Deadly Isle!" Bill gasped as he lunged forward.

With a mighty swipe,

CLUNK
a head was off –

and another,
until finally...

"We did it!" cried Bill. "Every last one of 'em down, me hearties!"

Joe shivered as he scanned the scattered skeletons.
Pieces of paper fluttered among the jumble of bones.
All the pieces of paper had writing on them and
two of them looked very useful indeed.

"I think the skeletons were hiding the
secret of the treasure," Joe said slowly.
"There are two useful clues here!"

I wish I'd
had a pirate cutlass
for that battle.

BOO HOO!

Treasure
in Creepy
Cavern

SHAKE
RATTLE
ROLL

Creepy
Cavern next
to tall palm
tree

DEM
BONES
DEM
BONES

FOR SALE
ONE FUNNY
BONE -
HARDLY USED

PARTY
TONIGHT

We are the
ISLE'S
GUARDS
Bones

Can you spot the useful clues?

19

Creepy Cavern

Bill read the clues and gave a low whistle. "So the treasure is in the Creepy Cavern?"

"And there's the tall palm tree next to it," Joe cried.

Sure enough, towering above the small shrubs and bushes was a palm tree, taller than all the rest. They set off...

...over a rickety rope bridge,

through squelchy quicksand,

across raging rivers,

until – Creepy Cavern! Bill was about to try the door, when suddenly, a man with a long beard jumped out at them...

"Yes sir," Joe stuttered in surprise.

Roger chuckled. "Then you'll need to unlock the door. You seem a polite young man so I'll help you. Somewhere nearby lie seven hidden objects like the ones on this scroll. Find them, place them in the holes in the door, and it will magically unlock."

Can you find all the objects they need?

Monster maze

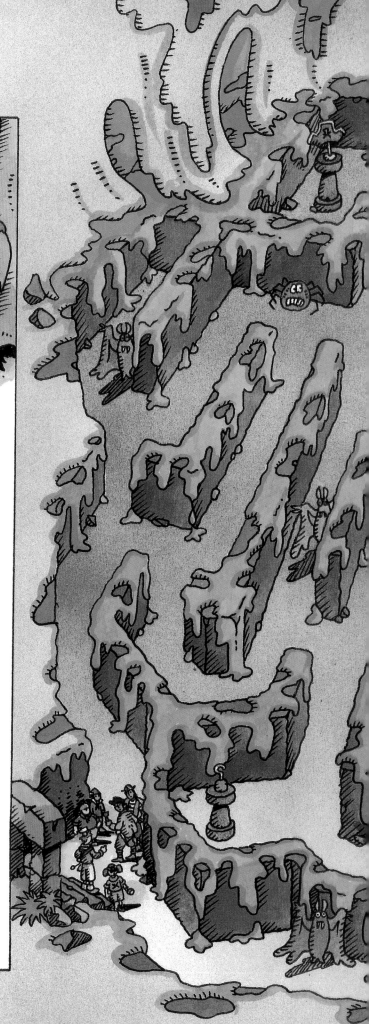

Thanks, Roger!

C-r-e-e-a-k. The door swung open and into Creepy Cavern they crept.

"Oh, I almost forgot!" Roger called. "A cyclops guards the trapdoor to the treasure. You'll need to find him some orange sea biscuits to munch so he'll let you through."

Joe shivered. A cyclops was bad enough, but he had thought of something else.

"If I remember my pirate geography lessons," he whispered to Bill, "Creepy Caverns are always home to Mighty Spiders and Vampire Bats. We must be careful which passage we take."

Can you find the way along the twisty passages to the trapdoor? Don't forget to look for the orange sea biscuits on the way!

Mermaid misery

The trapdoor opened to reveal a slide that led them down to an underground cave.

"What the...?" Bill began.

Hanging from the roof was the treasure chest! Dangling next to it was a key. But there were also mermaids, trapped in netted ponds, above which hung terrible sea monsters.

"Please help," cried a merboy. "One of these ropes leads to the key that will unlock us. But pull the wrong rope and those deadly sea monsters will spill out onto my five sisters. Can you set us free?"

Bill was puzzled. "Where do the ropes begin and end?"

"Look," said Joe. "The ropes tied to the rocks on the ground are all different shades. By matching them to the ropes hanging from the roof, I can see which rope leads where."

Can you find the right rope to release the key – and the rope to release the treasure chest too?

The treasure!

The key was freed and the chest was safely lowered down. Joe unlocked the mermaids and with a flash and a sparkle they swam out of the cave through an underground river. Joe and the crew followed them along the bank, carrying the chest with them. But to their dismay, they had walked straight into a trap.

"Ambush!" cried Captain Cutthroat. "All we had to do was follow ye scurvy dogs to the treasure and let ye do the hard work. Ha, it was almost too easy!"

But then Cutthroat yawned, as beautiful music filled the air. The mermaids were singing a magic tune and everyone began to feel very sleepy. Joe stole a quick glance at the little merboy.

"Quick," Joe whispered to Bill and the crew as Cutthroat's men began to nod off. "Find the shell headphones and cover your ears. Then you won't fall asleep."

Can you find the six shell headphones?

Yawn!

Shhh. Find six like these.

Pirate party

Quietly, Joe and the gang rowed back to the Salty Seal and opened the chest with the mermaids' key. Inside was the most amazing pirate treasure. In the middle of the jewels and glittery stuff there was a special message. It read,

"There's a gold cutlass here, treasure rare;
it can be claimed by one who dares.
If this pirate is clever, it will be his – forever."

"Well, if you can find it here, the gold cutlass is yours, Joe," said Bill. "Your quick thinking saved the day more than any swashbuckling skills. You have proved yourself a worthy pirate indeed."

Can you spot Joe's gold cutlass? Can you see what has happened to Cutthroat and his crew?

Three cheers for pirate Joe!

Pirate school

Back at school after his summer pirate adventure, Joe was proud to show off his new cutlass to all his friends.

"And I found these golden coins on my journey," he grinned. "There's one for each of you."

"Let's hear three cheers for pirate Joe," cried his teacher, and Joe's friends' voices raised the roof.

Go back through the book and spot the golden coin Joe collected for each pupil. There's one on every double page.

Answers

pages 4-5

pages 6-7

pages 8-9

Peg-leg Poll

Mophead Mick

One-eyed Jem

Rufus Redhead

Stripes

pages 10-11

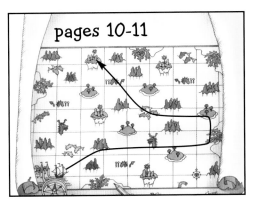

pages 12-13

Joe has spotted Cutthroat's Ghastly Galleon.

pages 14-15

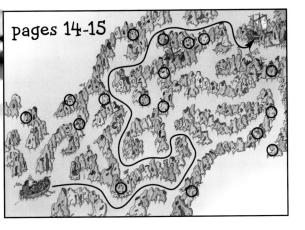

pages 16-17

1. First, we'll all row to the Ghastly Galleon,
2. where Bill, Rufus, Jem and Peg will climb aboard and set sail.
3. Meanwhile, Mophead and I will row behind the Galleon,
4. and when the ship is at sea, we will pick you up.
5. Then we'll all row back to Deadly Isle to look for the treasure.
6. We might meet Cutthroat and his crew there, but with their ship out to sea, they'll be stranded!

pages 18-19

The clues say:

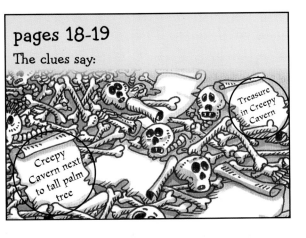

Treasure in Creepy Cavern

Creepy Cavern next to tall palm tree

pages 20-21

pages 22-23

pages 24-25

The red rope releases the treasure chest. The pink rope releases the key.

pages 26-27

pages 28-29

Cutthroat and his crew are stranded on Deadly Isle with the cyclops!

page 30

Did you spot the golden coin on each double page? (There isn't one on pages 2 and 3.)

Did you spot everything?

bald gull
skull
ghostly pirate
giant rat
jellyfish
octopus
stinging wasp
maggot
hungry crocodile
shark
spiky puffer fish
toothy starfish
angry porcupine

Did you spot Colin the parrot on every double page?

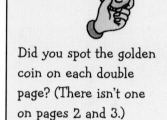

And did you find the mermaids' purses?

The list below shows you where the things to spot are hidden.

pages	objects	pages	objects
4-5	giant rat	18-19	skull
6-7	shark	20-21	stinging wasp
8-9	octopus	22-23	ghostly pirate
10-11	maggot	24-25	spiky puffer fish
12-13	hungry crocodile	26-27	angry porcupine
14-15	jellyfish	28-29	toothy starfish
16-17	bald gull		

First published in 2006 by Usborne Publishing Ltd., Usborne House, 83-85 Saffron Hill, London EC1N 8RT, England.

www.usborne.com

First published in America 2006
U.E. Printed in China.